Treasured Tales From
Beatrix Potter ™

THE ORIGINAL AND AUTHORIZED EDITIONS
by Beatrix Potter ™

New colour reproductions

BLOOMSBURY BOOKS
IN ASSOCIATION WITH
FREDERICK WARNE

BLOOMSBURY BOOKS IN ASSOCIATION WITH FREDERICK WARNE

Published by the Penguin Group
Penguin Books Ltd, 27 Wrights Lane, London W8 5TZ, England
Penguin Books USA Inc., 375 Hudson Street, New York, N.Y. 10014, USA
Penguin Books Australia Ltd, Ringwood, Victoria, Australia
Penguin Books Canada Ltd, 10 Alcorn Avenue, Toronto, Ontario, Canada M4V 3B2
Penguin Books (N.Z.) Ltd, 182-190 Wairau Road, Auckland 10, New Zealand

Penguin Books Ltd, Registered Offices: Harmondsworth, Middlesex, England

Bloomsbury Books, an imprint of the Godfrey Cave Group,
42 Bloomsbury Street, London WC1B 3QJ

First published by Frederick Warne & Co. 1987
This edition published 1993
1 3 5 7 9 10 8 6 4 2

ISBN 1 85471 315 9

Printed and bound in Great Britain by
William Clowes Limited, Beccles and London

Contents

The Tale of Tom Kitten .... page 5

The Tale of Mr. Jeremy Fisher ... 33

The Tale of Benjamin Bunny 61

The Tale of Pigling Bland 89

THE TALE OF
TOM KITTEN

ONCE upon a time there were three
little kittens, and their names were
Mittens, Tom Kitten, and Moppet.

They had dear little fur coats of
their own; and they tumbled about the
doorstep and played in the dust.

BUT one day their mother—Mrs. Tabitha Twitchit—expected friends to tea; so she fetched the kittens indoors, to wash and dress them, before the fine company arrived.

F IRST she scrubbed their faces (this
one is Moppet).

THEN she brushed their fur (this
one is Mittens).

THEN she combed their tails and whiskers (this is Tom Kitten).

Tom was very naughty, and he scratched.

MRS. TABITHA dressed Moppet and Mittens in clean pinafores and tuckers; and then she took all sorts of elegant uncomfortable clothes out of a chest of drawers, in order to dress up her son Thomas.

TOM KITTEN was very fat, and he had grown; several buttons burst off. His mother sewed them on again.

WHEN the three kittens were ready, Mrs. Tabitha unwisely turned them out into the garden, to be out of the way while she made hot buttered toast.

'Now keep your frocks clean, children! You must walk on your hind legs. Keep away from the dirty ash-pit, and from Sally Henny Penny, and from the pig-stye and the Puddle-Ducks.'

MOPPET and Mittens walked down the garden path unsteadily. Presently they trod upon their pinafores and fell on their noses.

When they stood up there were several green smears!

' LET us climb up the rockery, and sit on the garden wall,' said Moppet.

They turned their pinafores back to front, and went up with a skip and a jump; Moppet's white tucker fell down into the road.

TOM KITTEN was quite unable to jump when walking upon his hind legs in trousers. He came up the rockery by degrees, breaking the ferns, and shedding buttons right and left.

H E was all in pieces when he reached the top of the wall.

Moppet and Mittens tried to pull him together; his hat fell off, and the rest of his buttons burst.

WHILE they were in difficulties, there was a pit pat paddle pat! and the three Puddle-Ducks came along the hard high road, marching one behind the other and doing the goose step—pit pat paddle pat! pit pat waddle pat!

THEY stopped and stood in a row, and stared up at the kittens. They had very small eyes and looked surprised.

THEN the two duck-birds, Rebeccah and Jemima Puddle-Duck, picked up the hat and tucker and put them on.

MITTENS laughed so that she fell off the wall. Moppet and Tom descended after her; the pinafores and all the rest of Tom's clothes came off on the way down.

'Come! Mr. Drake Puddle-Duck,' said Moppet—'Come and help us to dress him! Come and button up Tom!'

M<small>R.</small> DRAKE PUDDLE-DUCK advanced in a slow sideways manner, and picked up the various articles.

B^{UT} he put them on *himself!* They fitted him even worse than Tom Kitten.

'It's a very fine morning!' said Mr. Drake Puddle-Duck.

A ND he and Jemima and Rebeccah
Puddle-Duck set off up the road,
keeping step—pit pat, paddle pat! pit
pat, waddle pat!

THEN Tabitha Twitchit came down the garden and found her kittens on the wall with no clothes on.

SHE pulled them off the wall, smacked them, and took them back to the house.

'My friends will arrive in a minute, and you are not fit to be seen; I am affronted,' said Mrs. Tabitha Twitchit.

SHE sent them upstairs; and I am sorry to say she told her friends that they were in bed with the measles; which was not true.

QUITE the contrary; they were not in bed: *not* in the least.

Somehow there were very extraordinary noises over-head, which disturbed the dignity and repose of the tea party.

A ND I think that some day I shall
have to make another, larger, book,
to tell you more about Tom Kitten!

A S for the Puddle-Ducks—they went into a pond.

The clothes all came off directly, because there were no buttons.

A ND Mr. Drake Puddle-Duck, and Jemima and Rebeccah, have been looking for them ever since.

THE TALE OF
MR. JEREMY FISHER

ONCE upon a time there was a frog called Mr. Jeremy Fisher; he lived in a little damp house amongst the buttercups at the edge of a pond.

THE water was all slippy-sloppy in
the larder and in the back passage.
But Mr. Jeremy liked getting his feet
wet; nobody ever scolded him, and he
never caught a cold!

HE was quite pleased when he looked out and saw large drops of rain, splashing in the pond—

'I WILL get some worms and go
fishing and catch a dish of minnows for my dinner,' said Mr. Jeremy
Fisher. 'If I catch more than five fish,
I will invite my friends Mr. Alderman
Ptolemy Tortoise and Sir Isaac Newton. The Alderman, however, eats
salad.'

MR. JEREMY put on a macintosh, and a pair of shiny goloshes; he took his rod and basket, and set off with enormous hops to the place where he kept his boat.

THE boat was round and green, and very like the other lily-leaves. It was tied to a water-plant in the middle of the pond.

MR. JEREMY took a reed pole, and pushed the boat out into open water. 'I know a good place for minnows,' said Mr. Jeremy Fisher.

MR. JEREMY stuck his pole into the mud and fastened his boat to it.

Then he settled himself cross-legged and arranged his fishing tackle. He had the dearest little red float. His rod was a tough stalk of grass, his line was a fine long white horse-hair, and he tied a little wriggling worm at the end.

THE rain trickled down his back, and for nearly an hour he stared at the float.

'This is getting tiresome, I think I should like some lunch,' said Mr. Jeremy Fisher.

HE punted back again amongst the
water-plants, and took some lunch
out of his basket.

'I will eat a butterfly sandwich, and
wait till the shower is over,' said Mr.
Jeremy Fisher.

A GREAT big water-beetle came up underneath the lily leaf and tweaked the toe of one of his goloshes.

Mr. Jeremy crossed his legs up shorter, out of reach, and went on eating his sandwich.

ONCE or twice something moved about with a rustle and a splash amongst the rushes at the side of the pond.

'I trust that is not a rat,' said Mr. Jeremy Fisher; 'I think I had better get away from here.'

MR. JEREMY shoved the boat out again a little way, and dropped in the bait. There was a bite almost directly; the float gave a tremendous bobbit!

'A minnow! a minnow! I have him by the nose!' cried Mr. Jeremy Fisher, jerking up his rod.

BUT what a horrible surprise! Instead of a smooth fat minnow, Mr. Jeremy landed little Jack Sharp the stickleback, covered with spines!

THE stickleback floundered about the boat, pricking and snapping until he was quite out of breath. Then he jumped back into the water.

AND a shoal of other little fishes
put their heads out, and laughed at
Mr. Jeremy Fisher.

A ND while Mr. Jeremy sat discon-
solately on the edge of his boat—
sucking his sore fingers and peering
down into the water—a *much* worse
thing happened; a really *frightful* thing
it would have been, if Mr. Jeremy had
not been wearing a macintosh!

A GREAT big enormous trout came up—kerpflop-p-p-p! with a splash— and it seized Mr. Jeremy with a snap, 'Ow! Ow! Ow!'—and then it turned and dived down to the bottom of the pond!

BUT the trout was so displeased with the taste of the macintosh, that in less than half a minute it spat him out again; and the only thing it swallowed was Mr. Jeremy's goloshes.

MR. JEREMY bounced up to the
surface of the water, like a cork
and the bubbles out of a soda water
bottle; and he swam with all his might
to the edge of the pond.

HE scrambled out on the first bank
he came to, and he hopped home
across the meadow with his macintosh
all in tatters.

'WHAT a mercy that was not a pike!' said Mr. Jeremy Fisher. 'I have lost my rod and basket; but it does not much matter, for I am sure I should never have dared to go fishing again!'

H E put some sticking plaster on his
fingers, and his friends both came
to dinner. He could not offer them
fish, but he had something else in his
larder.

SIR ISAAC NEWTON wore his
black and gold waistcoat,

AND Mr. Alderman Ptolemy Tortoise brought a salad with him in a string bag.

AND instead of a nice dish of minnows—they had a roasted grasshopper with lady-bird sauce; which frogs consider a beautiful treat; but *I* think it must have been nasty!

THE TALE OF BENJAMIN BUNNY

ONE morning a little rabbit sat on a bank.

He pricked his ears and listened to the trit-trot, trit-trot of a pony.

A gig was coming along the road; it was driven by Mr. McGregor, and beside him sat Mrs. McGregor in her best bonnet.

AS soon as they had passed, little Benjamin Bunny slid down into the road, and set off—with a hop, skip and a jump—to call upon his relations, who lived in the wood at the back of Mr. McGregor's garden.

THAT wood was full of rabbit holes; and in the neatest sandiest hole of all, lived Benjamin's aunt and his cousins—Flopsy, Mopsy, Cotton-tail and Peter.

Old Mrs. Rabbit was a widow; she earned her living by knitting rabbit-wool mittens and muffetees (I once bought a pair at a bazaar). She also sold herbs, and rosemary tea, and rabbit-tobacco (which is what *we* call lavender).

LITTLE Benjamin did not very much want to see his Aunt.

He came round the back of the fir-tree, and nearly tumbled upon the top of his Cousin Peter.

PETER was sitting by himself. He looked poorly, and was dressed in a red cotton pocket-handkerchief.

'Peter,'—said little Benjamin, in a whisper—'who has got your clothes?'

PETER replied—'The scarecrow in Mr. McGregor's garden,' and described how he had been chased about the garden, and had dropped his shoes and coat.

Little Benjamin sat down beside his cousin, and assured him that Mr. McGregor had gone out in a gig, and Mrs. McGregor also; and certainly for the day, because she was wearing her best bonnet.

PETER said he hoped that it would
rain.

At this point, old Mrs. Rabbit's voice
was heard inside the rabbit hole, call-
ing—'Cotton-tail! Cotton-tail! fetch
some more camomile!'

Peter said he thought he might feel
better if he went for a walk.

THEY went away hand in hand, and got upon the flat top of the wall at the bottom of the wood. From here they looked down into Mr. McGregor's garden. Peter's coat and shoes were plainly to be seen upon the scarecrow, topped with an old tam-o-shanter of Mr. McGregor's.

LITTLE Benjamin said, 'It spoils people's clothes to squeeze under a gate; the proper way to get in, is to climb down a pear tree.'

Peter fell down head first; but it was of no consequence, as the bed below was newly raked and quite soft.

IT had been sown with lettuces.
     They left a great many odd little
foot-marks all over the bed, especially
little Benjamin, who was wearing clogs.

LITTLE Benjamin said that the first thing to be done was to get back Peter's clothes, in order that they might be able to use the pocket-handkerchief.

They took them off the scarecrow. There had been rain during the night; there was water in the shoes, and the coat was somewhat shrunk.

Benjamin tried on the tam-o-shanter, but it was too big for him.

THEN he suggested that they should fill the pocket-handkerchief with onions, as a little present for his Aunt.

Peter did not seem to be enjoying himself; he kept hearing noises.

BENJAMIN, on the contrary, was perfectly at home, and ate a lettuce leaf. He said that he was in the habit of coming to the garden with his father to get lettuces for their Sunday dinner.

(The name of little Benjamin's papa was old Mr. Benjamin Bunny.)

The lettuces certainly were very fine.

PETER did not eat anything; he said he should like to go home. Presently he dropped half the onions.

LITTLE Benjamin said that it was not possible to get back up the pear-tree, with a load of vegetables. He led the way boldly towards the other end of the garden. They went along a little walk on planks, under a sunny red-brick wall.

The mice sat on their doorsteps cracking cherry-stones, they winked at Peter Rabbit and little Benjamin Bunny.

PRESENTLY Peter let the pocket-handkerchief go again.

THEY got amongst flowerpots, and frames and tubs; Peter heard noises worse than ever, his eyes were as big as lolly-pops!

He was a step or two in front of his cousin, when he suddenly stopped.

THIS is what those little rabbits saw
round that corner!

Little Benjamin took one look, and
then, in half a minute less than no
time, he hid himself and Peter and the
onions underneath a large basket....

THE cat got up and stretched herself, and came and sniffed at the basket.

Perhaps she liked the smell of onions!

Anyway, she sat down upon the top of the basket.

SHE sat there for *five hours.*

*   *   *   *   *

I cannot draw you a picture of Peter and Benjamin underneath the basket, because it was quite dark, and because the smell of onions was fearful; it made Peter Rabbit and little Benjamin cry.

The sun got round behind the wood, and it was quite late in the afternoon; but still the cat sat upon the basket.

A T length there was a pitter-patter, pitter-patter, and some bits of mortar fell from the wall above.

The cat looked up and saw old Mr. Benjamin Bunny prancing along the top of the wall of the upper terrace.

He was smoking a pipe of rabbit-tobacco and had a little switch in his hand.

He was looking for his son.

OLD Mr. Bunny had no opinion whatever of cats.

He took a tremendous jump off the top of the wall on to the top of the cat, and cuffed it off the basket, and kicked it into the green-house, scratching off a handful of fur.

The cat was too much surprised to scratch back.

WHEN old Mr. Bunny had driven the cat into the green-house, he locked the door.

Then he came back to the basket and took out his son Benjamin by the ears, and whipped him with the little switch.

Then he took out his nephew Peter.

THEN he took out the handkerchief
of onions, and marched out of the
garden.

WHEN Mr. McGregor returned about half an hour later, he observed several things which perplexed him.

It looked as though some person had been walking all over the garden in a pair of clogs—only the foot-marks were too ridiculously little!

Also he could not understand how the cat could have managed to shut herself up *inside* the green-house, locking the door upon the *outside*.

WHEN Peter got home, his mother forgave him, because she was so glad to see that he had found his shoes and coat. Cotton-tail and Peter folded up the pocket-handkerchief, and old Mrs. Rabbit strung up the onions and hung them from the kitchen ceiling, with the bunches of herbs and the rabbit-tobacco.

THE TALE OF
PIGLING BLAND

ONCE upon a time there was an old pig called Aunt Pettitoes. She had eight of a family : four little girl pigs, called Cross-patch, Suck-suck, Yock-yock and Spot; and four little boy pigs, called Alexander, Pigling Bland, Chin-chin and Stumpy. Stumpy had had an accident to his tail.

The eight little pigs had very fine appetites. 'Yus, yus, yus! they eat and indeed they *do* eat!' said Aunt Pettitoes, looking at her family with pride. Suddenly there were fearful squeals; Alexander had squeezed inside the hoops of the pig trough and stuck.

90

Aunt Pettitoes and I dragged him out by the hind legs.

Chin-chin was already in disgrace; it was washing day, and he had eaten a piece of soap. And presently in a basket of clean clothes, we found another dirty little pig. 'Tchut, tut, tut! whichever is this?' grunted Aunt Pettitoes. Now all the pig family are pink, or pink with black spots, but this pig child was smutty black all over; when it had been popped into a tub, it proved to be Yock-yock.

I went into the garden; there I found Cross-patch and Suck-suck rooting up

carrots. I whipped them myself and led them out by the ears. Cross-patch tried to bite me.

' Aunt Pettitoes, Aunt Pettitoes ! you are a worthy person, but your family is not well brought up. Every one of them has been in mischief except Spot and Pigling Bland.'

' Yus, yus ! ' sighed Aunt Pettitoes. ' And they drink bucketfuls of milk ; I shall have to get another cow ! Good little Spot shall stay at home to do the housework ; but the

others must go. Four little boy pigs and
four little girl pigs are too many altogether.'
' Yus, yus, yus,' said Aunt Pettitoes, ' there
will be more to eat without them.'

So Chin-chin and Suck-suck went away
in a wheel-barrow, and Stumpy, Yock-
yock and Cross-patch rode away in a cart.

And the other two little boy pigs, Pigling Bland and Alexander, went to market. We brushed their coats, we curled their tails and washed their little faces, and wished them good-bye in the yard.

Aunt Pettitoes wiped her eyes with a large pocket handkerchief, then she wiped Pigling Bland's nose and shed tears ; then she wiped Alexander's nose and shed tears ; then she passed the handkerchief to Spot. Aunt Pettitoes sighed and grunted, and addressed those little pigs as follows :

' Now Pigling Bland, son Pigling Bland, You must go to market. Take your brother Alexander by the hand. Mind your Sunday clothes, and remember to blow your nose '—(Aunt Pettitoes passed round the handkerchief again)—' beware of traps, hen roosts, bacon and eggs ; always walk upon your hind legs.' Pigling Bland, who

was a sedate little pig, looked solemnly at
his mother, a tear trickled down his cheek.

Aunt Pettitoes turned to the other—
'Now son Alexander take the hand '—
'Wee, wee, wee!' giggled Alexander—
'take the hand of your brother Pigling
Bland, you must go to market. Mind—'
'Wee, wee, wee!' interrupted Alexander

again. ' You put me out,' said Aunt Pettitoes—'Observe sign-posts and milestones;
do not gobble herring bones—' ' And
remember,' said I impressively, ' if you
once cross the county boundary you
cannot come back. Alexander, you are not
attending. Here are two licences permit-
ting two pigs to go to market in Lancashire.
Attend, Alexander. I have had no end of
trouble in getting these papers from the
policeman.' Pigling Bland listened
gravely; Alexander was hopelessly vola-
tile.

I pinned the papers, for safety, inside
their waistcoat pockets; Aunt Pettitoes
gave to each a little bundle, and eight
conversation peppermints with appropri-
ate moral sentiments in screws of paper.
Then they started.

Pigling Bland and Alexander trotted
along steadily for a mile; at least Pigling
Bland did. Alexander made the road half
as long again by skipping from side to side.

He danced about and pinched his brother,
singing—

'This pig went to market, this pig stayed at home,
'This pig had a bit of meat—

let's see what they have given *us* for dinner,
Pigling?'

Pigling Bland and Alexander sat down
and untied their bundles. Alexander gob-

bled up his dinner in no time; he had already eaten all his own peppermints. 'Give me one of yours, please, Pigling.' ' But I wish to preserve them for emergencies,' said Pigling Bland doubtfully. Alexander went into squeals of laughter. Then he pricked Pigling with the pin that had fastened his pig paper; and when Pigling slapped him he dropped the pin, and tried to take Pigling's pin, and the papers got mixed up. Pigling Bland reproved Alexander.

But presently they made it up again, and trotted away together, singing—

' Tom, Tom, the piper's son,
    stole a pig and away he ran !
' But all the tune that he could play,
    was " Over the hills and far away !" '

' What's that, young sirs? Stole a pig? Where are your licences ? ' said the policeman. They had nearly run against him round a corner. Pigling Bland pulled out his paper; Alexander, after fumbling, handed over something scrumply—

' To $2\frac{1}{2}$ oz. conversation sweeties at three farthings '—' What's this ? This ain't a

licence.' Alexander's nose lengthened visibly, he had lost it. ' I had one, indeed I had, Mr. Policeman! '

' It's not likely they let you start without. I am passing the farm. You may walk with me.' ' Can I come back too?' inquired Pigling Bland. ' I see no reason, young sir ;

your paper is all right.' Pigling Bland did not like going on alone, and it was beginning to rain. But it is unwise to argue with the police; he gave his brother a peppermint, and watched him out of sight.

To conclude the adventures of Alexander—the policeman sauntered up to the house about tea time, followed by a damp subdued little pig. I disposed of Alexander in the neighbourhood; he did fairly well when he had settled down.

Pigling Bland went on alone dejectedly; he came to cross-roads and a sign-post— 'To Market Town, 5 miles,' 'Over the Hills, 4 miles,' 'To Pettitoes Farm, 3 miles.'

Pigling Bland was shocked, there was little hope of sleeping in Market Town, and to-morrow was the hiring fair; it was deplorable to think how much time had

been wasted by the frivolity of Alexander.

He glanced wistfully along the road towards the hills, and then set off walking obediently the other way, buttoning up his coat against the rain. He had never wanted to go; and the idea of standing all by himself in a crowded market, to be stared at, pushed, and hired by some big strange farmer was very disagreeable—

' I wish I could have a little garden and grow potatoes,' said Pigling Bland.

He put his cold hand in his pocket and felt his paper, he put his other hand in his

other pocket and felt another paper—
Alexander's! Pigling squealed; then ran
back frantically, hoping to overtake Alexander and the policeman.

He took a wrong turn—several wrong
turns, and was quite lost.

It grew dark, the wind whistled, the
trees creaked and groaned.

Pigling Bland became frightened and cried 'Wee, wee, wee! I can't find my way home!'

After an hour's wandering he got out of the wood; the moon shone through the clouds, and Pigling Bland saw a country that was new to him.

The road crossed a moor; below was a wide valley with a river twinkling in the moonlight, and beyond, in misty distance, lay the hills.

He saw a small wooden hut, made his way to it, and crept inside—'I am afraid it *is* a hen house, but what can I do?' said Pigling Bland, wet and cold and quite tired out.

'Bacon and eggs, bacon and eggs!' clucked a hen on a perch.

' Trap, trap, trap! cackle, cackle, cackle! ' scolded the disturbed cockerel. ' To market, to market! jiggetty jig! ' clucked a broody white hen roosting next to him. Pigling Bland, much alarmed, determined to leave at daybreak. In the meantime, he and the hens fell asleep.

In less than an hour they were all awakened. The owner, Mr. Peter Thomas Piperson, came with a lantern and a hamper to catch six fowls to take to market in the morning.

He grabbed the white hen roosting next to the cock; then his eye fell upon Pigling Bland, squeezed up in a corner. He made a singular remark—' Hallo, here's another! '—seized Pigling by the scruff of the neck, and dropped him into the hamper. Then he dropped in five more dirty, kicking, cackling hens upon the top of Pigling Bland.

The hamper containing six fowls and a young pig was no light weight; it was taken down hill, unsteadily, with jerks. Pigling, although nearly scratched to

pieces, contrived to hide the papers and peppermints inside his clothes.

At last the hamper was bumped down upon a kitchen floor, the lid was opened, and Pigling was lifted out. He looked up, blinking, and saw an offensively ugly elderly man, grinning from ear to ear.

' This one's come of himself, whatever,' said Mr. Piperson, turning Pigling's pock-

ets inside out. He pushed the hamper into a corner, threw a sack over it to keep the hens quiet, put a pot on the fire, and unlaced his boots.

Pigling Bland drew forward a coppy stool, and sat on the edge of it, shyly warming his hands. Mr. Piperson pulled off a boot and threw it against the wainscot at the further end of the kitchen. There was a smothered noise—'Shut up!' said Mr. Piperson. Pigling Bland warmed his hands, and eyed him.

Mr. Piperson pulled off the other boot

and flung it after the first, there was again a curious noise—' Be quiet, will ye?' said Mr. Piperson. Pigling Bland sat on the very edge of the coppy stool.

Mr. Piperson fetched meal from a chest and made porridge. It seemed to Pigling that something at the further end of the kitchen was taking a suppressed interest in the cooking, but he was too hungry to be troubled by noises.

Mr. Piperson poured out three platefuls : for himself, for Pigling, and a third—after glaring at Pigling—he put away with much scuffling, and locked up. Pigling Bland ate his supper discreetly.

After supper Mr. Piperson consulted an almanac, and felt Pigling's ribs ; it was too late in the season for curing bacon, and he grudged his meal. Besides, the hens had seen this pig.

He looked at the small remains of a flitch, and then looked undecidedly at Pigling. 'You may sleep on the rug,' said Mr. Peter Thomas Piperson.

Pigling Bland slept like a top. In the morning Mr. Piperson made more porridge; the weather was warmer. He looked to see how much meal was left in the chest, and seemed dissatisfied—' You'll likely be moving on again?' said he to Pigling Bland.

Before Pigling could reply, a neighbour, who was giving Mr. Piperson and the hens a lift, whistled from the gate. Mr. Piperson hurried out with the hamper, enjoining Pigling to shut the door behind him and not meddle with nought; or 'I'll come back and skin ye!' said Mr. Piperson.

It crossed Pigling's mind that if *he* had asked for a lift, too, he might still have been in time for market.

But he distrusted Peter Thomas.

After finishing breakfast at his leisure, Pigling had a look round the cottage; everything was locked up. He found some potato peelings in a bucket in the back kitchen. Pigling ate the peel, and washed

up the porridge plates in the bucket. He
sang while he worked—

    ' Tom with his pipe made such a noise,
        He called up all the girls and boys—
    ' And they all ran to hear him play
        "Over the hills and far away!"'

Suddenly a little smothered voice chimed in—

'Over the hills and a great way off,
The winds shall blow my top knot off!'

Pigling Bland put down a plate which he was wiping, and listened.

After a long pause, Pigling went on tip-toe and peeped round the door into the front kitchen. There was nobody there.

After another pause, Pigling approached the door of the locked cupboard, and snuffed at the keyhole. It was quite quiet.

After another long pause, Pigling pushed a peppermint under the door. It was sucked in immediately.

In the course of the day Pigling pushed in all the remaining six peppermints.

When Mr. Piperson returned, he found Pigling sitting before the fire; he had brushed up the hearth and put on the pot to boil; the meal was not get-at-able.

Mr. Piperson was very affable; he slapped Pigling on the back, made lots of porridge and forgot to lock the meal chest. He did lock the cupboard door; but without properly shutting it. He went to bed early, and told Pigling upon no account to disturb him next day before twelve o'clock.

Pigling Bland sat by the fire, eating his supper.

All at once at his elbow, a little voice spoke—'My name is Pig-wig. Make me more porridge, please!' Pigling Bland jumped, and looked round.

A perfectly lovely little black Berkshire pig stood smiling beside him. She had twinkly little screwed up eyes, a double chin, and a short turned up nose.

She pointed at Pigling's plate; he hastily gave it to her, and fled to the meal chest. 'How did you come here?' asked Pigling Bland.

'Stolen,' replied Pig-wig, with her mouth full. Pigling helped himself to meal without scruple. 'What for?' 'Bacon, hams,' replied Pig-wig cheerfully. 'Why on earth don't you run away?' exclaimed the horrified Pigling.

'I shall after supper,' said Pig-wig decidedly.

Pigling Bland made more porridge and watched her shyly.

She finished a second plate, got up, and looked about her, as though she were going to start.

'You can't go in the dark,' said Pigling Bland.

Pig-wig looked anxious.

'Do you know your way by daylight?'

'I know we can see this little white house from the hills across the river. Which way are *you* going, Mr. Pig?'

'To market—I have two pig papers. I might take you to the bridge; if you have

no objection,' said Pigling much confused
and sitting on the edge of his coppy stool.
Pig-wig's gratitude was such and she asked
so many questions that it became embar-
rassing to Pigling Bland.

He was obliged to shut his eyes and
pretend to sleep. She became quiet, and
there was a smell of peppermint.

'I thought you had eaten them,' said Pigling, waking suddenly.

'Only the corners,' replied Pig-wig, studying the sentiments with much interest by the firelight.

'I wish you wouldn't; he might smell them through the ceiling,' said the alarmed Pigling.

Pig-wig put back the sticky peppermints into her pocket; 'Sing something,' she demanded.

'I am sorry ... I have toothache,' said Pigling much dismayed. 'Then I will sing,' replied Pig-wig. 'You will not mind if I say iddy tidditty? I have forgotten some of the words.'

Pigling Bland made no objection; he sat with his eyes half shut, and watched her.

She wagged her head and rocked about, clapping time and singing in a sweet little grunty voice—

' A funny old mother pig lived in a stye, and three little
  piggies had she;
' (Ti idditty idditty) umph, umph, umph! and the little
  pigs said, wee, wee!'

She sang successfully through three or four verses, only at every verse her head nodded a little lower, and her little twinkly eyes closed up.

' Those three little piggies grew peaky and lean, and lean
  they might very well be;
' For somehow they couldn't say umph, umph, umph!
  and they wouldn't say wee, wee, wee!
' For somehow they couldn't say—

Pig-wig's head bobbed lower and lower, until she rolled over, a little round ball, fast asleep on the hearth-rug.

Pigling Bland, on tip-toe, covered her up with an antimacassar.

He was afraid to go to sleep himself; for the rest of the night he sat listening to the chirping of the crickets and to the snores of Mr. Piperson overhead.

Early in the morning, between dark and daylight, Pigling tied up his little bundle and woke up Pig-wig. She was excited and half-frightened. 'But it's dark! How can we find our way?'

'The cock has crowed; we must start before the hens come out; they might shout to Mr. Piperson.'

Pig-wig sat down again, and commenced to cry.

'Come away Pig-wig; we can see when we get used to it. Come! I can hear them clucking!'

Pigling had never said shuh! to a hen in his life, being peaceable; also he remembered the hamper.

He opened the house door quietly and shut it after them. There was no garden; the neighbourhood of Mr. Piperson's was all scratched up by fowls. They slipped away hand in hand across an untidy field to the road.

The sun rose while they were crossing the moor, a dazzle of light over the tops of the hills. The sunshine crept down the slopes into the peaceful green valleys, where little white cottages nestled in gardens and orchards.

'That's Westmorland,' said Pig-wig.
She dropped Pigling's hand and commenced to dance, singing—

'Tom, Tom, the piper's son,
  stole a pig and away he ran!
'But all the tune that he could play,
  was "Over the hills and far away!"'

'Come, Pig-wig, we must get to the
bridge before folks are stirring.' 'Why do
you want to go to market, Pigling?'
inquired Pig-wig presently. 'I don't want;
I want to grow potatoes.' 'Have a pepper-

mint?'said Pig-wig. Pigling Bland refused quite crossly. 'Does your poor toothy hurt?' inquired Pig-wig. Pigling Bland grunted.

Pig-wig ate the peppermint herself and followed the opposite side of the road. 'Pig-wig! keep under the wall, there's a man ploughing.' Pig-wig crossed over, they hurried down hill towards the county boundary.

Suddenly Pigling stopped; he heard wheels.

Slowly jogging up the road below them
came a tradesman's cart. The reins flapped
on the horse's back, the grocer was reading
a newspaper.

'Take that peppermint out of your
mouth, Pig-wig, we may have to run. Don't
say one word. Leave it to me. And in sight
of the bridge!' said poor Pigling, nearly
crying. He began to walk frightfully lame,
holding Pig-wig's arm.

The grocer, intent upon his newspaper,
might have passed them, if his horse had
not shied and snorted. He pulled the cart
crossways, and held down his whip.

'Hallo! Where are *you* going to?'—
Pigling Bland stared at him vacantly.

'Are you deaf? Are you going to
market?' Pigling nodded slowly.

'I thought as much. It was yesterday.
Show me your licence?'

Pigling stared at the off hind shoe of the
grocer's horse which had picked up a stone.

The grocer flicked his whip—'Papers?
Pig licence?' Pigling fumbled in all his
pockets, and handed up the papers. The
grocer read them, but still seemed dissatisfied. 'This here pig is a young lady; is
her name Alexander?' Pig-wig opened

her mouth and shut it again; Pigling coughed asthmatically.

The grocer ran his finger down the advertisement column of his newspaper— 'Lost, stolen or strayed, 10s. reward.' He looked suspiciously at Pig-wig. Then he stood up in the trap, and whistled for the ploughman.

'You wait here while I drive on and speak to him,' said the grocer, gathering up the reins. He knew that pigs are slippery; but surely, such a *very* lame pig could never run!

'Not yet, Pig-wig, he will look back.'
The grocer did so; he saw the two pigs
stock-still in the middle of the road. Then
he looked over at his horse's heels; it was
lame also; the stone took some time to
knock out, after he got to the ploughman.

'Now, Pig-wig, NOW!' said Pigling
Bland.

Never did any pigs run as these pigs ran! They raced and squealed and pelted down the long white hill towards the bridge. Little fat Pig-wig's petticoats fluttered, and her feet went pitter, patter, pitter, as she bounded and jumped.

They ran, and they ran, and they ran down the hill, and across a short cut on level green turf at the bottom, between pebble beds and rushes.

They came to the river, they came to the bridge—they crossed it hand in hand— then over the hills and far away she danced with Pigling Bland!